PIPER MORGAN
TO THE RESCUE

DON'T MISS ANY OF PIPER'S ADVENTURES!

Piper Morgan Joins the Circus

Piper Morgan in Charge!

COMING SOON:

Piper Morgan Makes a Splash

ALSO BY STEPHANIE FARIS:

30 Days of No Gossip

25 Roses

PIPER MORGAN

TO THE RESCUE

BY STEPHANIE FARIS

ILLUSTRATED BY LUCY FLEMING

ALADDIN

New York   London   Toronto   Sydney   New Delhi

ALADDIN
An imprint of Simon & Schuster Children's Publishing Division
1230 Avenue of the Americas, New York, New York 10020
First Aladdin hardcover edition November 2016
Text copyright © 2016 by Stephanie Faris
Illustrations copyright © 2016 by Lucy Fleming
Also available in an Aladdin paperback edition.
For information about special discounts for bulk purchases, please contact Simon & Schuster Special Sales at 1-866-506-1949 or business@simonandschuster.com.
The Simon & Schuster Speakers Bureau can bring authors to your live event. For more information or to book an event contact the Simon & Schuster Speakers Bureau at 1-866-248-3049 or visit our website at www.simonspeakers.com.
Book designed by Laura Lyn DiSiena
The text of this book was set in New Baskerville.
Manufactured in the United States of America 1016 FFG
2 4 6 8 10 9 7 5 3 1
Library of Congress Control Number 2016953050
ISBN 978-1-4814-5715-6 (hc)
ISBN 978-1-4814-5714-9 (pbk)
ISBN 978-1-4814-5716-3 (eBook)

For Rhett, the coolest little dude
I've ever met

CHAPTER ★ 1 ★

I've always really wanted a dog of my own.

I've never had one before, but I've always wanted one. Mom always said it wasn't the right time, but there's never a bad time to have a puppy in your life.

My nanna has a cute little dog named Oreo. He's black and white and loves to have dance parties with me. I *love* Oreo. I got to hang out with him all the time when we lived with Nanna for a little bit. But Mom got a new job, so I don't get to live with Oreo anymore. We just moved into a new place in Ohio.

My mom has worked lots of jobs. She's worked in a circus and a school. And each time, I got to help out in my own special way too.

Now we were going to work where doggies and kitties came when they didn't have homes. Mom said it was called a pet rescue. She was going to help the boss, who owned lots and lots of pet places in Ohio. Mom was going to be what's called an "assistant director."

Plus, not only did we get to go somewhere new . . . it sounded like I might be able to be around a lot of really cute animals. . . . It was another great adventure.

I hadn't always liked new adventures. At first I was scared about going to new places. But every time we went to a new place, I got to make new friends and have new fun experiences. I've performed in a circus with other kids called Little Explorers, and was a helper bee at a principal's office. And now we were at my mom's new job. It was summer, so I didn't have to go to school. That was good. It meant we could work at lots of jobs all summer and then maybe get a new job near a really good school that would be my forever home.

But first, I would be hanging out with animals. Lots and lots of animals.

"Can we keep one, please, please, please?" I asked my mom on the way to the rescue shelter to meet her new boss.

One "please" doesn't get you as much

as three of them. Most of the time, grown-ups don't say yes even to three pleases, but sometimes they do. So you should always try.

Please, please, *please*!

"No pets," Mom said. "Not until we get settled somewhere."

"Maybe this will be our new home," I said. "I like Ohio."

I did miss Nanna, though. Nanna was two hours from here. That was a long, long way, but not too long. Mom said we could still go visit on our days off, though, which were every Sunday and sometimes Monday.

"Maybe it will be," Mom said. "But we're just helping out right now while the owner opens a new store, remember?"

I knew that, but I thought I might like this job best of all the ones we had done so far. My most favorite part of the circus was the elephant named Ella. I made friends after that and they were the best part, but I still liked the elephant.

Dogs and cats are even better than elephants. You know why? Because you can have them in your house. They can even sleep on your bed if your parents will let you.

I decided this was going to be the for-ever job. I'd do an extra-good job and then Mom would let us have a puppy dog of our very own. Because life is just so much better if you have a puppy sleeping next to you.

Fur Fact #1

Almost half of all dog owners let their dogs sleep in bed with them at night. Some pet owners don't like it though. They think it's best that their pets sleep in their own beds at night, just like kids sleep in their own beds.

But did you know that back in the old days, people in Australia slept with their dogs to keep warm? Two dogs were used for colder nights, and if it was really, really cold, it would be a "three-dog night."

Those were the days when people had to sleep outside, though. And they didn't have blankets like we do now. So if you tell your parents you need a dog to keep you warm at night, you might want to leave those last two things out of your talk.

CHAPTER
★ 2 ★

AS soon as we pulled up to the rescue center, all we could see were happy dog faces and wagging tails. Dogs were everywhere! It was the coolest thing ever.

There was a woman standing outside the door holding about a billion leashes. Each one had a dog attached to it. There were little dogs and big dogs and black dogs and tan dogs. There were dogs with lots of fur and dogs without much fur at all. I wanted to hug them all!

"Mom!" I called out as we got closer. She could see the same thing I was seeing, but she didn't look as excited as I felt.

"Piper, stay with me," Mom ordered.

I looked over at her and wanted to ask why. But the look on her face told me, *Don't push me, young lady*. I'd seen that look lots of times.

Oh, wait . . . I bet I knew what was going on here. Mom didn't want me to pet the dogs because she knew I'd want to take one home with us. I was just supposed to meet the nice person who owned this place, and then Mom would (maybe) take me for ice cream.

"You must be Julie Morgan," the woman with the dogs said to my mother as we got closer.

"Yes," Mom said, giving her big smile. She stepped in front of me, putting her hand on my shoulder to make sure I stayed nearby. A bunch of puppies that were close to Mom came rushing toward her, but the woman held on to the leashes really tightly.

"Let me get these dogs inside," the woman said. "I'll be back in just a second."

The woman pulled out some keys and unlocked the front door. A big sign on the front window said BARK STREET, with the words WHERE PETS AND OWNERS MEET. A big white bone was behind it. I liked this place already.

"Stay away from the dogs," Mom warned. "Some may bite."

That was all she got in before the woman came back and opened the door for us. "Come on in," she said. "I'm Pamela. What's your name?"

She was talking to me, but she was using a weird voice. Like she was talking to a puppy or something.

"Piper," I said. "I'm seven."

I said that last part because questions like, "How old are you?" and, "What grade are you in?" almost always followed the name question.

"Seven!" Pamela exclaimed. "My favorite dog is seven years old too. Do you want to meet her?"

I looked at Mom. She had just told me to stay away from the dogs, but I really,

really wanted to meet Pamela's favorite dog.

"I'm a little nervous about Piper and the dogs," Mom said. "Is it safe?"

"Oh, of course!" Pamela said. "A lot of them are in their cages right now. Come with me."

She waved for both of us to follow, and we went through a door into a big room with stacks of cages. As we walked by, a few of the dogs inside ran to their cage doors, giving us excited barks of hello. I saw tons of the prettiest animal faces I'd ever seen. There were cats in some of the cages, dogs in others. I even recognized some from outside.

"So do any of these guys have new owners yet?" I asked. Mom had told me that animals came here to wait for homes. She said people came here and picked out which animals they wanted to take home.

"Not right now," Pamela said. "But we're going to the park this afternoon, and we're taking a bunch of them to see if they might find their forever home. Do you want to go with us?"

I nodded, my eyes really big. But then I looked at my mom, who still looked all nervous.

"I was going to have you stay with the neighbors," she said.

"This would be more fun," I said. "I want to help find homes for these dogs and cats. Please, Mom. Please?"

I didn't add the third "please." I didn't

have to. I could tell my mom was going to say yes even after the first "please." You know why? Because Mom wanted to go to the park too. And I had a plan: Operation Puppy Plan, that is!

Fur Fact #2

Pet shelters help dogs and cats find homes. The nice people working there will take care of them until the animals find their forever homes.

Some shelters have more than dogs and cats. You can get rabbits, hamsters, or turtles, too!

Before you get a pet, you should make sure you can take care of it. You have to feed your pets at least twice every single day and keep water in their dishes. If you have a dog, you'll have to take him out to potty. If you have a cat, you'll have a litter box that has to be cleaned at least once a day.

So when your parents say pets are a lot of work, think about all these things.

CHAPTER
★ 3 ★

It was time to try to put my Operation Puppy Plan in action! But the first thing I needed to do was pick the puppy I wanted.

After loading some of the dogs into the big Bark Street van, we made our way to a little park in the center of town. Pamela, Mom, and a high school helper named Sandie helped to set up the cages and some tables with all the papers people would need to fill out in order to get a pet.

I started walking around the cages to take a look at who was up for adoption. They were all so cute. But I stopped right in front of one dog in particular, who stared at me with big brown puppy-dog eyes.

I was in love.

I took a look at his little nameplate, which Pamela had made for all the dogs who were up for adoption. His name was Gonzo, and right under his name, Pamela had put that he was a Maltese. That sounded like he was very, very important.

Right next to Gonzo was another dog named Beanie. Beanie was a big female dog that they said was a mastiff. A mastiff is big. Did I mention how big she was? She came all the way up to my belly button. That was a big dog.

Beanie also was a little slobbery. Yuck!

I decided right then and there that I was more of a "little" dog person. They aren't as slobbery and smelly as big dogs. I decided I wanted a dog like Gonzo or Oreo.

"Hello there!" a woman said when I was near the cage. "Someone said you're helping out the Bark Street people. Could I see the little white dog?"

She wanted to see Gonzo, but I was standing in front of the cage so nobody could see him. We'd been at this park for a whole fifteen minutes, and I'd stayed in front of this cage the whole time.

"He's not for adoption," I said quickly.

The woman's face changed. She looked disappointed. "Oh. Okay."

I felt bad after she walked away. My mom had told me never, ever to tell a fib. Fibs were like . . . little lies that weren't big ones. Lies were important. I wasn't supposed to tell those, either.

Another woman walked up right after. She walked around me and looked inside the cage. Most people walked past when they saw me standing in front of it, but this woman must have really wanted to see.

"How is the little Maltese, behavior-wise?" the woman asked. "He looks like a cutie-pie, and my kids would love him!"

I thought about telling another fib—saying that Gonzo liked to bite. But I couldn't keep fibbing. That wasn't nice at all.

"Same as the others," I finally said. "He's sweet. But did you see the mastiff?"

I opened Beanie's cage, hoping she'd reach in and pet her. The woman shook her head.

"That dog is way too big for us," she explained. She pointed at Gonzo again.

"May I see him, please?" the woman asked.

My job was to pull the dogs out and let

people hold them. I was also supposed to watch and make sure the dogs didn't get away. I didn't know if I could catch one if it did run away, but I figured the grown-ups would all help.

I didn't move. I didn't want the nice lady to look at my little Gonzo.

Gonzo was going home with *me.*

"What's going on over here, Piper?"

Mom's voice came from behind the lady, who was now frowning. The woman smiled at my mom, and I knew I'd lost.

Within seconds, Gonzo was in the woman's arms and she was signing the papers to take him home. I wasn't even sure how it happened, but I wanted to cry. Gonzo was supposed to be mine. I wanted to tell everyone there how upset I was about it.

"Is something wrong, Piper?" Mom asked when I stood in front of the next cage. There were cute puppies inside, but none of them was Gonzo.

I shook my head. I could feel tears coming, but I didn't want to have to explain everything that happened. I did kind of fib, after all.

"Where's Beanie?" Pamela asked.

We turned to look. Beanie's cage was wide open. It was also *empty*.

"Piper?" Mom asked. "Did you leave Beanie's cage open?"

Fur Fact #3

Dogs come in lots of different shapes and sizes. Some people like really big dogs while others like teeny-tiny ones. Many of us don't care—dogs are cute no matter what the size.

But there are big differences between big and small dogs. Small dogs don't take up much space. They're also easy to carry around.

Big dogs can be scary to kids, but they aren't always dangerous. It all depends on the type of dog. You have to learn all about a dog before taking it home.

What's your favorite kind of dog?

CHAPTER ★ 4 ★

Dinnertime was my favorite time with Mom. We sat at the table and ate and talked about our day. It was nice when we lived with Nanna, because we got to have dinner with her. But I liked having Mom to myself too.

"This is nice," I told Mom. I gave her a big smile.

My mom didn't smile at me. She was still a little not-happy because I'd let

Beanie get out. She didn't get far—it's hard for a mastiff to sneak away without someone noticing. But Mom still said it showed I had a "responsibility problem," and we needed to talk about it.

Only we weren't talking. Mom was just frowning all the time.

"Mrs. Dorris is nice," I commented.

Mrs. Dorris was my new babysitter. I'd been on extra-good behavior since the park a couple of days ago, but my mom thought it might be better if I didn't go to Bark Street until I learned the whole "responsibility" thing. Only then could I be with the dogs and cats again.

"Mom?" I asked after another bite or two of my sketti. That was what my best friend, Dania, called spaghetti in kindergarten. I still liked to call it that because it reminded me of her.

"Yes?" Mom asked. She was eating her sketti too.

"Can I go to work with you tomorrow?"

Mom sighed. "I told you, Piper, I can't watch you and the dogs," she said. "I really think you need to be with Mrs. Dorris next door while I'm at work."

"But I'll help. I promise."

"You kept talking nonstop about some dog named Gonzo," Mom said. "I can't have you getting attached to all the dogs. Besides, I might get in trouble if I have you there every day with me."

I frowned. "Miss Pamela likes me," I said. "I can tell she does."

"It's not that, Piper," Mom said. "It's just that it is not professional if I keep bringing you in every day, even though I know she likes you a lot. Especially with all the dogs and some of the equipment in the shelter. We don't want you to get hurt."

I knew that word "professional." Grown-ups used it a lot. It basically meant "not fun at all."

"Can I come see the dogs for just a couple of hours?" I asked. "Please, please, please, *please*?"

That was four "pleases." *No* mom could resist four "pleases."

But then Mom said something all grown-ups say when they want to stop the questions.

"We'll see."

Fur Fact #4

Piper Morgan's advice on how to get your parents to buy a pet:

#1 PROMISE to HELP take care of it.

#2 LEARN LOTS about THE KIND OF PET YOU LIKE. FIND ONE THAT'S NICE AND CUTE AND NOT TOO MESSY.

#3 DROP LITTLE HINTS about WHAT YOU'VE LEARNED about THAT TYPE OF PET.

#4 MAKE A LIST OF ALL THE THINGS YOU'LL DO TO TAKE CARE OF THE PET. SIGN it.

#5 LET YOUR PARENTS SEE ALL THE PETS at THE SHELTER. WHEN THEY SEE HOW CUTE THEY ALL ARE, YOU WON'T EVEN HAVE TO SAY "PLEASE" ONCE!

CHAPTER
★ 5 ★

Saturdays were the best days of all. On those days, Mrs. Dorris couldn't watch me. I thought Mom was going to get the nice lady across the hall from our apartment to watch me, but it "didn't work out." So do you know what that means?

I got to go to Mom's work. Only "temporarily" until she could find another sitter. But it didn't matter to me.

The whole drive to the pet rescue was

a long, long lecture. Mom gave me a list of rules:

1) No running.

2) No playing.

3) No letting dogs out of their cages.

4) No talking to customers without permission.

5) No getting in the way.

There were other rules, but I knew them already. It was like when my mom worked in a school and I was told to stay in a seat in the principal's office. That hadn't worked out so well. But this time I was going to behave, I promised. This time I wanted to show Mom that I could be a good helper. Then she'd let me come to work with her every day. And I would be that much closer to having a puppy of my very own.

Maybe this puppy called Taffy. Taffy was my favorite dog ever, ever, *ever.* Well, maybe except Oreo, but Oreo was at Nanna's house. I was hoping maybe we could bring Taffy home with us soon.

We walked in the door, and I went to the little table in the corner. I'd brought a book about puppies, and I was going to pretend to read it while Mom worked. Miss Pamela was behind the counter, talking on the phone, and she kept talking while Mom put her purse up.

"Of course," Miss Pamela was saying into the phone. "It's just— Well, we have so much going on today. I'd need to—"

She stopped talking and looked at me. Her eyes squinched a little. She was thinking.

"We can do it!" the woman said. "Come on over. We'll see you at ten."

I looked from Miss Pamela to Mom. Something good was going to happen. I could tell.

As it turned out, I wouldn't be hearing that right away. Miss Pamela and Mom stood behind the counter whispering to each other. For a long time. I wanted to know what they were saying, but they were whispering, so I couldn't hear.

"Piper, would you like to help out today?" Miss Pamela asked.

I'd forgotten about the way she always talked to me like I was a puppy, in that high-pitched, silly voice. But I decided not to worry about that because she was about to give me a super-awesome assignment.

"We have a big group coming here

today," Miss Pamela continued. "We promised them a while back that if they'd come look at some of our animals, we wouldn't charge the fee."

"Miss Pamela needs for you to help show them around," Mom said. "But you need to make sure you show them all the dogs. No saving the cute ones for yourself."

Miss Pamela looked at my mom. "Do you guys want a dog? Because I could—"

"Thank you, but not right now," Mom interrupted. "Maybe in a little while."

I wanted to say, *Yes-yes-yes!* But my mom would give a big frowny face at that. It would be one of those *Young lady, I told you not to do this* faces, even though saying yes to a dog wasn't against the rules.

Begging for a dog was, though.

I was still frowning over that thought

when I realized I wasn't in my chair any-more. I'd walked to the counter to talk to Miss Pamela. Mom had told me to stay in that chair.

I went back over and sat down, trying to be as quiet as I could be. I'd do this until Miss Pamela told me what she wanted me to do next. Miss Pamela got really busy. The phone was ringing and people were coming in, and she and Mom were gone in the back for a super-long time. I sat there, staring out the window and bounc-ing up and down in my chair, until finally a big pink bus that read BIG RIVER BAPTIST CHURCH pulled up. It wasn't as big as my school bus, but it still looked big.

When the bus door opened, I wanted to jump out of my chair. All of a sudden, people were pouring out of that bus. There were more people coming out of there than seats in the bus, I was pretty sure.

Then they were coming in the front door. And there was nobody at the front desk. It was just me in the corner.

I went to the door where the puppies were and opened it. I was yelling, "Miss Pamela," when I saw her standing right there. But she had lots of people around her.

"Is everything okay?" Miss Pamela asked.

"Yes, but the people are here," I said. I pointed at the big crowd of people.

"Oh goodness."

She looked around, but there were puppies everywhere. My mom was way down the hall, talking to a couple who were holding two puppies. She looked kind of busy too.

"Could you let them know I'll be right with them?" Miss Pamela asked. "Thank you, dear."

I went back outside, feeling all excited. I got to be a real worker.

Instead of going to the lobby, I went behind the counter. That was what a real worker would do. I climbed up on the counter and stood, facing the group of people on the other side of it.

"Listen up!" I shouted, because there was lots and lots of talking. They wouldn't have heard me if I didn't yell. "I'm Piper Morgan."

They all looked at me. They were all grown-ups and one little girl. She was standing in front of an older man.

"I'm Shelby Sheridan," she said.

I smiled at her. She didn't smile back.

Sometimes it took a little while for people to become friends. I learned that when I was in the circus and when I was the helper bee at the school.

"It'll be just a minute," I said. Then I started to jump down. I was going to go talk to Shelby to see if we could be friends.

"Can I ask a question?" a lady near the front asked.

I was already thinking about a way to jump down, but her question surprised me. I didn't know any answers, but I liked this. It felt like I was a real employee.

"Do you have any little dogs?" she asked.

I smiled. "Lots of them," I said. "There are Chihuahuas and terriers and something called a minpin."

I still didn't know what a minpin was, but I liked the way the name rhymed. Plus, she was a cute little dog. She wasn't my favorite dog, though. My favorite dog was Taffy.

"Are any of them puppies?" someone else asked.

The questions went on and on. And the coolest part was that I knew a lot of the answers. I knew them from seeing the dogs at the park and listening to Mom talk. By the time Miss Pamela came out, I think I sounded like a real expert.

"Thank you, Piper," Miss Pamela said. She sounded really, truly impressed. "Piper is our little helper today. She'll take you back to where all the cages are while I help this lovely couple with their new friend."

I looked over, sure that "lovely couple" would be holding one of the little dogs I loved. Instead they had one of the cute little kittens. I let out the breath I'd been holding, then hopped down from the counter to show all my new friends where the cutest pets in the world were.

Fur Fact #5

Little dogs are cute and fun, but big dogs are the most popular. Retrievers are the most popular dogs and they're sixty-five pounds or more! German shepherds are really popular too, and they can be seventy-five pounds or more.

Why are these dogs so loved? Because they're sweet and they behave.

But small dogs are great too. Beagles and Yorkshire terriers are the most popular small dogs, followed by boxers and dachshunds.

All puppies are little when they're born. But some people can say you can tell how big a dog will get by looking at its paws. If a little puppy has big paws, watch out!

CHAPTER ★ 6 ★

I really was a helper for Miss Pamela. It was awesome.

The church brought bunches of people and they all followed me into the room where the pets were. Mom was still in the back—now they were looking at cats. A couple of people headed back to the cats, but most stayed with me.

"Here they are," I said, waving my hand in the air dramatically. I learned that while working in the circus. You waved when you were showing things off.

"They're so cu-u-ute!" one of the women exclaimed. She was looking at one of the poodles. I breathed a big sigh of relief. My favorite dog, Taffy, was the Yorkie—that's short for Yorkshire terrier, by the way.

"Those ones are the best!" I gushed. Then I opened the door to the cage to show them.

"Can I see this one?" one of the other women asked. She was pointing to the one with bigger dogs in it.

I looked at the woman with the poodles. She seemed to have it all under control. I opened the other cage.

Then someone else wanted a cage opened.

I looked at the door. Where was Miss

Pamela? I needed her. Everyone wanted to see puppies and some of the cats at once, and there was only one me. Plus, how could I guard my favorite doggy's cage if I was helping everyone?

I was helping with a golden retriever's cage when I saw—*oh no!*—that girl Shelby was standing in front of my Yorkie's cage. I whipped open the cage for the retriever people, then rushed over to her.

"Can I see this one?" she asked.

"You don't want to see her," I said.

Shelby frowned, looking inside the cage again. "Why not?" she asked.

"She pees everywhere," I said quickly. "Floors, countertops, her cage . . ."

I knew that because Mom had complained about it last night. I thought it was cute, but Mom said that was why we could never have her as a dog. I was hoping she'd change her mind.

"So?" Shelby said. "I want to see her. I want to hold her. I want to see her NOW!"

People had stopped playing with their dogs and were now staring at us. We were making a scene.

"Okay," I said, mostly because I had no other choice. "But don't be mad at me if she pees on you."

I opened the cage and pulled Taffy out. I pulled her to my chest and held her for a long, long time. I'd only held her once before—when I stopped by here with Mom after day care so she could pick something up. Then my mom wouldn't let me hold her long because we "didn't have time for that."

Now I didn't have time either. Shelby

was reaching for Taffy, and if I didn't let her go, she might hurt her.

"Not like that," I said. "You have to support her bottom, too."

Shelby looked annoyed, but she was holding Taffy by her front legs and it was all awkward and stuff. I put my own left hand on Taffy's bottom to push her closer to Shelby's chest.

"I know how to hold a dog," Shelby snapped.

I was going to argue with her more, but then I remembered I wanted to be Shelby's friend. It had been a long time since I'd had a really good friend. All the other kids at Mrs. Dorris's house were practically babies. I wanted to hang around someone my own age.

"I'm sorry," I said. I stepped back. "Her name's Taffy. She's my favorite."

The girl looked at me, and this time she didn't have the mean look on her face that she had before. She actually smiled at me. "She is really cute," she said.

"What do you have there?" the old man who had been standing behind Shelby in the lobby asked. He'd squeezed through the crowd until he was standing beside Shelby.

"Her name is Taffy," the girl said. "She's mine."

"She pees a lot," I said.

I wasn't sure where that came from. When she said, "She's mine," though, my chest had gotten all squeeze-y and I felt like I couldn't breathe. I wanted Taffy to come home with me.

"Ewww!" Shelby suddenly squealed. She pulled Taffy way away from her and I thought she was going to drop her. I reached out to hold the puppy just in case.

"Oh my," the old man said with a chuckle. And then I saw it. A yellow spot on Shelby's perfectly white T-shirt. Uh-oh.

"I told you," I said.

"She tinkled on me!" Shelby said very loudly. People were staring again.

"I'll take her," I said. This was the not-so-fun part of the job—cleaning up after the animals. They weren't as cute when they made a mess!

"That's okay," the old man said. "We'll find a different dog. What about this little one over here?"

Yay! She didn't want Taffy after all. This was the best thing to ever happen to anyone ever.

"Okay, everyone," Miss Pamela called out from the doorway before I could show Shelby and the man more dogs. "If any of you are ready, please bring your new pets to the front counter so we can fill out the papers."

Only a few people had pets. The rest

of the animals were back in their cages. I followed Shelby and the old man toward the lobby.

"Grandpop, can I please, please, please have Taffy?" Shelby begged. "I'll make sure she won't make a mess, I promise."

"We'll see," he said.

"But what if someone else buys her?" Shelby asked.

Suddenly, she turned to look at me. I was still holding Taffy and hoping nobody would notice. Maybe I could even take her home with me. Mom would see how cute she was and want to keep her forever and ever.

"Can you please make sure nobody buys Taffy?" Shelby asked. "Please? I'll be your best friend forever."

I nodded. Who can say no to a best

friend forever? Plus, it was easy to promise I would never let anyone else buy Taffy. No way would that happen . . . because she would be mine.

Fur Fact #6

Dogs are like humans . . . only different. Here are a few ways dogs are different from us:

#1 DOGS SWEAT THROUGH THEIR PAWS AND SOMETIMES THEIR NOSES.

#2 A DOG'S WHISKERS CAN SENSE EVEN THE SMALLEST CHANGE IN AIR DIRECTION.

#3 WHEN DOGS DRINK WATER, THEY BEND THEIR TONGUES AND LIFT THE WATER UP TO THEIR MOUTHS ALL ROLLED UP.

#4 WHEN A PUPPY IS BORN, HE'S BOTH BLIND AND DEAF. HE ALSO HAS NO TEETH.

#5 A DOG'S NOSE IS SO UNIQUE, IT COULD BE USED TO IDENTIFY HIM . . . LIKE HUMAN FINGERPRINTS!

#6 A DOG'S EARS ARE VERY SENSITIVE, WHICH IS WHY RAIN, THUNDER, AND FIREWORKS UPSET THEM SO MUCH.

CHAPTER
★ 7 ★

Dinner was different when it was just Mom and me. Nanna was what they call "retired," which I think means that you're tired after working for lots and lots of years. Nanna says, "That's about right." When you're retired, you have time to do the stuff you love. And Nanna likes to cook.

Every night at Nanna's house, we had a homemade dinner with vegetables that she made herself. She didn't even use a can. Mom is all about the can. Tonight we're having ravioli, and dinner rolls that look like a smile.

I think that's yummy. But sometimes I miss Nanna's cooking. Shhhh. Don't tell Mom that.

"I was very proud of you today," Mom said after watching me stuff a whole ravioli in my mouth.

I couldn't say anything to that, so I just chewed my ravioli.

"You were so mature, helping everyone find dogs," Mom continued. "I may have been wrong about having you at the rescue shelter. You may be the perfect person to help out there."

That made me smile the biggest smile you can smile with a part-eaten ravioli in your mouth.

I chewed. And thought. And chewed and thought some more. By the time I swallowed, I knew what I wanted to ask.

"Can we bring Taffy home with us?" I asked.

Now Mom had a ravioli in her mouth. In her case it was only part of one, though. She didn't look so happy anymore when she finished chewing.

"Piper, what did I say about dogs?"

I'd thought about that. I'd thought about it since Shelby left the store today. I had a good argument for it too.

"You said we aren't in one place enough to have a dog, but I just want to bring Taffy home for a few days. Maybe this weekend. And I'll feed her and take her outside on her leash to pee and you won't have to do anything, I promise. Please, please, please?"

"I'll think about it," Mom said, spearing the other half of her ravioli piece with her fork.

"I'll think about it" isn't a good thing. "I'll think about it" is something a grown-up says to make you stop asking. But "I'll think about it" isn't the end.

"I'll think about it" means there is still time to change your mom's mind.

Fur Fact #7

Dogs are popular pets, but cats are pretty popular too. In fact, there are more cats as pets than dogs. Here are some fun facts about cats:

#1 GROWN-UP CATS MEOW ONLY TO COMMUNICATE WITH HUMANS.

#2 MOST CATS LIKE TO BE PETTED, SO PET AWAY!

#3 CATS CAN'T TASTE SWEET FOODS.

#1 CATS PURR WHEN THEY'RE HAPPY. CATS PURR WHEN THEY'RE UPSET. CAN YOU TELL WHETHER YOUR CAT IS HAPPY OR UPSET?

#5 THERE ARE SIXTEEN TO TWENTY-FOUR WHISKERS ON EVERY CAT. GO AHEAD— COUNT THEM!

CHAPTER
★ 8 ★

I was trying to play a game of Duck, Duck, Goose with the rest of the kids at Mrs. Dorris's day care when my mom came to get me. It wasn't going well. Especially since some of them couldn't really walk yet.

Mrs. Dorris was a sweet woman with a round face and big, smiley eyes. She and Mom didn't normally talk for long times, but they did today. I was listening closely.

"Piper is just a delight," I heard Mrs. Dorris say. "Look at her."

They both turned to look at me, so I gave them a big smile. Then I guess they figured out I could hear them. They started talking about grown-up stuff.

When Mom and I were in the car, I thought about the good things Mrs. Dorris had said. "I'm doing a really good job as Mrs. Dorris's helper," I pointed out.

"You're her helper?" Mom asked, sounding all surprised.

"Yes. I help make lunches and sit quietly during naps. I also keep the other kids entertained when Mrs. Dorris needs to 'sit a spell.'"

Mom laughed. Then she said, "It sounds like you're a good little helper."

"I am," I said. "I know I can help out with a puppy, too!"

I let Mom think about that for a minute. I wanted her to decide that good helpers could help at the rescue shelter too. I wanted to spend more time with Taffy.

"I've been thinking," Mom said. "If it's okay with Miss Pamela, maybe we could take Taffy home with us for a couple of days. We could do that with different puppies until they find homes."

"Really?" I asked. I bounced up and down on my seat, so excited I could barely sit still. This was the Best. News. Ever.

"Don't get too excited," Mom warned. "We still have to get Miss Pamela's approval."

I was still too excited to stay in my seat. I

waited until the car was in its parking space and pushed on my seat-belt button before Mom even had the keys out. I was reaching for the door handle when Mom reminded me I couldn't cross the parking lot without her anyway, so what was my hurry?

I hopped up and down in place to try to get some of my excitement out. It didn't work. I wanted to run to the building and grab Taffy up in my arms and never, ever let her go. But I took a deep breath and held my mom's hand as we walked slowly— *so slowly*—to the building where little Taffy would be waiting.

Once we were safe on the sidewalk, I let go of Mom's hand and ran. I pulled open the door fast and rushed inside. Miss Pamela wasn't at the front desk, so I ran straight to the back. Straight to Taffy's cage.

Only Taffy wasn't in there.

The cage was empty.

"Where is she?" I asked in a panicky voice.

Miss Pamela was down at the end with the cats. She hurried over when she saw the look on my face.

"Who?" Miss Pamela asked when she got to me. "Are you okay, Piper?"

I didn't answer that. I just pointed at the empty cage.

"Taffy's gone!" I yelled.

"Oh." Miss Pamela put her hand on her chest like she was able to breathe again. "I thought something was really wrong."

"Something *is* wrong. Taffy's gone!" I said again, because she must not have been able to hear me. "She's gone! It's a huge emergency."

That was when Miss Pamela's face changed. "Taffy found a new home," Miss Pamela said gently. "It's great news."

No. It wasn't. Taffy was supposed to find *my* home.

"You were attached to Taffy, weren't you?" Miss Pamela said softly. She looked at the cage, thought a minute, and then turned back to me. "I used to get attached to the animals here too, and it was really hard. Almost every dog and cat you see here will leave us. That's the goal. We want to get them out of these cages and into a good home. Understand?"

"But I want them to come to *my* home," I said. "We wanted to take Taffy to stay with us."

Tears were coming to my eyes now, and Miss Pamela's face got even softer. I probably should have told her that Mom and I were only going to borrow Taffy and Mom might not have even let me keep her. She probably wouldn't. This was the better thing for Taffy, but it wasn't the better thing for me.

"I didn't know you wanted to adopt a pet," Miss Pamela said. "We can find you a great pet. The perfect pet for you and your

mom. We'll just decide what you want and we'll look around."

"Pamela?" Mom called from the front. "Mr. Sheridan is here to see you."

"Mr. Sheridan!" Miss Pamela said. She looked down at me. "He's Taffy's new owner. Do you want to meet him?"

I wanted to shake my head no. It would just make me sad. But maybe the new owner would see how sad I was and decide to bring Taffy back. Or maybe . . .

Maybe . . .

Maybe he was bringing Taffy back!

"Okay," I said. Miss Pamela was holding her hand out and I took it. She led me out to the lobby, where an older man was waiting.

Hey! I knew that old man. He was Shelby's grandfather!

"I remember this young lady," the man Shelby had called Grandpop said. "This is exactly whom I came here to see."

The grandfather had a big, smiley face. Big, smiley faces brought big, smiley news. Like that they were bringing puppies back to see you.

"I wanted to thank you for showing us Taffy," he said. "She has made Shelby so happy. You see, Shelby's been really sad lately because she lost her best friend."

"Lost her?" I asked. "Like a lost dog?"

The old man laughed. "No, like a friend who says she doesn't want to be your best friend anymore."

Oh. I knew how that felt. I was always trying to ask people to be my best friend and it was really hard. Since leaving home, I'd only had one real best friend—at the circus—and I'd had to leave her.

"It's hard to find best friends," I said.

"But Taffy is helping Shelby feel not as lonely," Shelby's grandfather said. "So, thank you."

The grandfather turned toward the counter and started to say something to Mom, who was standing behind it. But then he turned back to me, and for just a second, I thought he might tell me I could keep Taffy, after all. As a gift. For being such a nice helper.

Instead he said, "I just thought of something. Why don't you come over for a sleepover? You can hang out with Taffy and get to know Shelby a little better."

Hang out with Taffy? And a sleepover? This day had just gotten bunches better.

Fur Fact #8

Best friends are great, but animals can be even better. Dogs are the *best* best friends of all. Here are a few reasons why:

#1 IF ANYONE EVER COMES TO YOUR DOOR, YOUR DOG WILL PROTECT YOU AND BARK AT THE PERSON. EVEN IF THE PERSON IS JUST SELLING COOKIES OR DELIVERING PACKAGES.

#2 DOGS ARE ALWAYS THERE FOR YOU. THEY'LL HANG OUT WITH YOU ON A SATURDAY AND WATCH MOVIES OR SIT BESIDE YOU WHILE YOU READ.

#3 DOGS ARE ALWAYS HAPPY TO SEE YOU COME HOME, EVEN IF YOU'VE ONLY BEEN GONE FOR A FEW MINUTES.

#1 PETTING A DOG IS GOOD FOR YOUR HEALTH. STUDIES HAVE PROVEN IT.

CHAPTER ★ 9 ★

I knew instantly that Shelby would be the *best* best friend ever because her house was not far from mine. You could count to a hundred and you'd be there. That's how close she was.

I had my best PJs in my backpack, along with my favorite books and my toothbrush and toothpaste. I also had some clothes to wear home the next day. It had been a long time since I'd had a sleepover, so Mom had to remind me to take my toothbrush.

My heart was all fluttery as I walked up the steps to her house. Mom was standing beside me, so I shouldn't have been nervous, but I was. What if Shelby didn't like me? What if she was mean?

"Well?" Mom asked, making me realize I'd been standing there for a long time. "Are you going to ring the doorbell?"

The doorbell glowed like a night-light. I wanted to reach up and press it, but I knew when I did, that door would open and I'd know, once and for all, whether Shelby was going to be nice to me or not.

"Don't be nervous, Piper," Mom said, reaching over and pressing the button. "I'm sure you will have a great time."

Ding-dong.

BARK-BARK-BARK-BARK-BARK.

I looked up at Mom with a big smile on my face. Taffy! I'd almost forgotten that I got to spend the night with Taffy, too. Even if Shelby was really mean to me, I'd have Taffy.

The door started to open, then shut again.

"Shelby, come get this dog before she runs out into the street!" a man's voice yelled out.

I took a deep breath. I heard footsteps on the other side of the door, then a few seconds later the door opened. Shelby's grandpop was smiling at us.

"Little Miss Piper!" the man said with a big grin. "Welcome! I know you girls are going to have a lot of fun."

He looked down at the spot next to him, then got a confused look on his face. Then he looked behind him. I could see little Taffy's head popping around the old man's arm, and I wanted to reach out and pet her.

"Shelby!" the old man gasped. "What are you doing hiding back there?"

"I don't know," a timid voice squeaked.

"Come on out and say hi to Piper," the grandfather said. Then he looked at me.

Slowly, Shelby peeked around her grandfather. I saw the top of her head, then her forehead, then finally her whole body.

I gave her a big smile. She stood near her grandfather. She didn't smile back yet, holding Taffy really close.

"I think she'll be in good hands here," Shelby's grandfather said to Mom once I was inside. Shelby's grandpa stepped out onto the porch. That meant they were leaving Shelby and me alone.

That was when the nervous stuff really happened.

Luckily, we had Taffy to make it easier.

"You can pet her if you want," Shelby said. She pulled her away from her chest a little.

I reached out and pet Taffy's back. That made me feel happy. Taffy closed her eyes and sniffed the air, so I could tell she liked it.

"You want to see Taffy's bedroom?" Shelby asked.

I looked up at Shelby, surprised. "She has her own bedroom?" I asked.

"Yes, well . . . sort of. She mostly spends time with me, though. Come on."

We went up a really tall staircase with lots of stairs. They seemed like they were going to go up forever and ever. When we got to the top, we went to the left. First we saw Taffy's room. It was a little room with white walls and toys all over the floor. The perfect room for a dog.

Then we went to Shelby's room, which was *magnificent*. There was lots of pink and prettiness. There was a big pink fluffy rug in the center of the room and a matching pink bedspread. There was also a big picture of a puppy.

"That's my old dog, Jake," Shelby explained. "He died last year." Jake was a different kind of dog from Taffy, but he wasn't the kind of dog I'd seen before. He looked like a nice dog. I thought for a minute.

"It must be hard when a dog dies," I said.

She nodded. "I miss him so much. But Taffy helps."

I saw how happy Taffy looked. If dogs could smile, I was pretty sure Taffy would have the biggest smile of all dogs ever.

"Want to hold her?" Shelby asked.

I smiled. "Can I?"

"Of course."

She handed Taffy over and the puppy settled into my arms. It felt so nice to hold Taffy again, but I was sad in a way because I knew Taffy couldn't be mine. Ever. She had a new home.

"Where does Taffy sleep?" I asked.

"Right here next to me," Shelby said, patting the bottom left corner of the bed. I pictured Taffy all snuggled up at night, curled in a ball at Shelby's feet.

That was when I knew. Shelby was happy.

I saw a big dog bone and a couple of toys scattered around the room. Taffy had a really fun life here. She would have had an amazing life with us, too, but . . .

That was when I realized what my mom had been saying. We moved lots right now and that wasn't good for a dog. All I'd been thinking about was me and how happy a dog would make me. I hadn't thought about the dog. Or that other people needed a dog maybe more than I did.

Miss Pamela was right. What we did at the rescue shelter was important. We helped dogs and cats find good homes—homes like this one. Homes with people who would give them a comfy place to sleep and a room full of toys. When Mom and I settled into our forever home, we'd get a dog from a rescue shelter like the one Taffy came from. Then we'd give that dog the best life ever.

Until then, I'd just have to have lots of sleepovers with Shelby.

Fur Fact #9

Pets should be treated like princesses (or princes). They should have a comfy home and owners who love them and pet them every day. But there are some things owners do that might not be so good for a pet. They include:

#1 Letting the pet ride in a car without a seat belt (pets should be in a crate).

#2 Letting the pet eat human food.

#3 Hugging the pet (animals don't understand or like hugs).

#4 Giving the pet too many treats or too much pet food.

#5 Not letting the pet explore when you go for a walk.

CHAPTER ✦10✦

There was a new animal at the rescue shelter. She was a pretty Persian kitten and I loved her.

She wasn't Shelby's favorite. Shelby's favorite was a little corgi named Mack, short for Mackenzie. We got to name him because he came in one day when we were working there. After the best sleepover ever, Shelby and I had become best friends. Now we worked at the shelter together and sometimes even had sleepovers at my apartment.

"Shelby, Piper, come out here!" Miss Pamela said one afternoon when we were cleaning cages. "I need your help."

We looked at each other and smiled. Helping was our favorite thing ever. It made us feel grown up.

A lady was standing at the counter. Miss Pamela introduced her as Mrs. Maley.

"Mrs. Maley wants to adopt a new little furry friend," Miss Pamela said. "Why don't you show her around?"

I held open the door and Mrs. Maley walked through. She smiled down at us as I showed her my favorite dogs and cats. I even showed her Tootsie, my favorite kitten.

"This is the best one of all," I said, pulling Tootsie out of her cage. "She's Persian.

She's from Europe. Persian cats are really quiet."

I was attached, but that was the funny part. Now I knew that I was just taking care of the animals until a nice person came in who would take them home and take really good care of them. That made me feel happy.

In fact, it was always easier to show guests my favorite dogs and cats. They almost always picked them to go home.

"I think I'll take her home with me," Mrs. Maley said. "She seems like the perfect cat to keep me company."

I smiled at Shelby, who was watching, wide eyed, behind me. She still couldn't believe that every time I picked a favorite, that was the next pet to be adopted.

Once Mrs. Maley and her new kitten

were out the door, Miss Pamela told us that Mrs. Maley was lonely, and hoped having a pet in the house would help.

I smiled. Tootsie would definitely help Mrs. Maley be less lonely. I knew she would.

Later I saw Miss Pamela come through the adoption area with a new dog, one a woman had brought in. This one had big, sweet eyes that made me just want to give it a big hug.

"His name is DJ," Miss Pamela said. "Do you want to help me find a good home for him?"

Did I? But first I wanted to play with him and walk him and pet him lots and lots.

"Why don't you and Shelby walk him close by?" Miss Pamela asked. "Maybe you'll meet some people who will give him a good home."

I liked that idea. "And maybe we could take him to the park Sunday too and we can all talk to some people?" I asked. "There are usually families there. Maybe we could find him a home with kids."

Miss Pamela smiled. "That sounds like a plan to me. His treats are over there."

I grabbed a dog's leash and potty bags, then put the leash on him. I had this part down. My job was to go out in front of the store and walk him on his leash—always where Mom or Miss Pamela could see me. Then I'd come back in and trade him for another dog that needed to go potty.

We were walking DJ on the little patch of grass near the store when Mom pulled into a parking space. She'd left to get milk shakes for everyone. She got out of the car

and watched us for a second before walking over to us.

"New dog?" Mom asked.

"Yep," Shelby said. "His name is DJ."

"He's my new favorite," I added.

"We all know what that means," Mom said with a laugh. "Looks like DJ will have a new home soon."

As we followed Mom back toward the building, guiding our new four-legged friend, I realized it had been a long, long time since I'd asked Mom if we could have a new puppy. I had something better than a forever furry friend. I had a forever *human* friend, and that was good enough for me!

Turn the page for a sneak peek at
Piper's next adventure:

PIPER MORGAN MAKES A SPLASH

The funny man on the TV was yelling at me.

"Summer is coming! It's time to buy a pool! We have inground pools, above-ground pools, hot tubs, and tanning beds!" As he showed us all the different pools, the salesman was wearing a funny float in the shape of a flamingo. He looked like he was ready for a fun pool day!

I pressed the minus button on the

remote control. That much noise wasn't good for anybody!

"Piper? What did I tell you about watching too much TV?" Mom yelled. She marched into the living room and blocked my view of the TV.

I thought for a minute. I stared up at the ceiling. I think staring at the ceiling helps me think better sometimes.

"Um . . ."

I had nothing.

"That's enough TV for today," she said. "We have a lot to do. I need you to get dressed."

My mom has a new job. Again. So "a lot to do" means doing errands and going food shopping for the week so my nanna doesn't have to cook for us all the time. We started staying with Nanna when Mom got a job at a school nearby, and then moved away when Mom worked at Bark Street, a pet rescue place. But now Mom has a job that is only two minutes away from Nanna's house, and it is *magnificent*.

"Magnificent" is a new word I learned. It means "really good," or "excellent." I'm trying it out. *Mag-nif-i-cent!*

My mom has worked a lot of different jobs as we try to find our own forever home. It is hard sometimes to leave behind the new friends I make, but it also means I get to have new adventures all the time, like being in the circus, helping at a school principal's office, and helping at the pet shelter with lots of really cute puppies! (The principal's office is more adventurous than you'd think!)

Mom told me I was dawdling and she

wasn't going to wait around all day, missy. Plus she had a surprise for me. Surprises were good. Surprises maybe meant we were stopping by my favorite store with all the smell-good soaps and lotions.

"Come on, Oreo," I called out to Nanna's dog, a little black-and-white terrier that Nanna says is a "terror." He reminded me of my favorite little dog at the pet rescue center, Taffy. I ran down the hall to my room with Oreo on my heels. If I was really good, Mom might let me come help out at her new job again!

SPLASH FACT #1

Grown-ups always say watching too much TV is bad for you. How do you know if you're watching too much TV, though? Here are some clues:

#1 YOU THINK ABOUT YOUR FAVORITE TV SHOW ALL THE TIME.

#2 YOU KNOW MORE ABOUT THE PEOPLE YOU WATCH ON TV THAN ABOUT YOUR OWN FRIENDS.

#3 YOU SKIP FUN THINGS BECAUSE YOU DON'T WANT TO MISS YOUR FAVORITE SHOW.

#4 YOU ASK YOUR MOM TO BRING YOU THINGS SO YOU DON'T HAVE TO TAKE YOUR EYES OFF THE SCREEN.

#5 YOU COMPARE ALL YOUR FRIENDS TO CHARACTERS ON YOUR FAVORITE SHOWS.